Marcel is a French mouse, and a detective. He has lots of
friends in Paris. One of them is Céline. She paints
pictures and is very beautiful. Céline's home is at the
Louvre. Marcel often goes there for dinner. One evening
in May he arrives with some pink flowers. There is a
guard at the door. "I don't know him," Marcel thinks.
"He must be new." Then he walks inside.

The two friends eat, drink and talk all evening. Céline
shows Marcel her new paintings. They talk about their
summer holiday in Los Angeles. They laugh, play jazz
records and tell lots of stories. Then at 11 o'clock
Marcel puts on his coat. "It's late," he says. "I must go
home." Two minutes later he leaves. "Good night," says
Céline. Then she closes her front door.

Marcel walks across the floor. He is very happy. Then he stops. The room is dark, but he can see something. What is it? A man? A man with a long knife? *Yes*! Suddenly Marcel's mouth is very dry. He runs to the wall. Then, after five seconds he looks again. This time he can see the man's face. "It's that new guard," he thinks. "And he's . . . he's stealing the Mona Lisa!"

3

Next to the thief there is a black bag. Two minutes later the Mona Lisa is inside it. The thief smiles and picks up the bag. But a second later he puts it down again. "Car keys," he says, and begins to look in all his pockets. "All right – this is it," Marcel thinks. "It's now or never." He runs along the wall very fast, climbs up the tall, black bag, and jumps inside it.

At the bottom of the bag Marcel can see a face. The
Mona Lisa's face. She is smiling at him. "Now what?"
he asks her. There is no answer, but at that moment the
bag starts to move. Marcel can hear lots of noises: a
motor starts – traffic goes by – a radio plays. Then the
bag suddenly stops. Marcel climbs the painting and
looks out. "A railway station!"

Five minutes later the Louvre 'guard' gets on a train. He sits next to a thin man in sunglasses and a white jacket. "Have you got it, Antoine?" the thin man asks. "Yes," the guard answers. After that the train starts and there is a lot of noise. "Oh no! Now I can't hear them," Marcel thinks. But he *can* hear one or two words. "Italy", for example, and "all those cats".

"Cats!" Marcel looks at the Mona Lisa. His eyes are two big saucers. "But cats *kill* mice," he thinks. "They *eat* them. And where are we going in Italy? Rome? Milan? Naples? . . ."

But at that moment Antoine puts the bag under the seat.

"Now I *really* can't hear," Marcel thinks.

Then he goes to sleep and has a very bad dream.

Early next morning the sun is shining. Marcel opens his
eyes and sees the Mona Lisa. Then he remembers where
he is. He runs up the painting and looks at Antoine and
Henri. "Good," he thinks. "They're asleep." Ten
seconds later, Marcel is standing at the window. He can
see a small village and some mountains. Then a sign
goes by: a hundred and eighty kilometres to Venice!

Two hours later Antoine and Henri are on a gondola.
"Look," says Antoine and laughs. He shows Henri a
newspaper story. It says, 'THIEVES TAKE DA VINCI
PAINTING'. Henri says, "Be quiet!" and turns to the
boatman. "Do you see that big palace on the left?"
"Signor Spandini's house?" "Yes. Stop there."
Inside the bag Marcel hears every word.

An old woman answers the front door. "Come in," she says to the two thieves. "Signor Spandini is waiting for you." She takes them to a big, dark room. A fat man is sitting behind a desk. "Have you got it?" he asks. "Yes, Boss," Henri answers. The bag is beside him. "I can't stay in here," Marcel thinks. He jumps out of the bag and hides behind a chair.

"Good," he thinks. "Now I can . . ." But then he goes
cold. "Cats!" There are seven, eight – no *nine* of them
in the room. Suddenly Marcel remembers Henri's words
– "all those cats." Then he remembers his dream on the
train. What can he do? Where can he go?
But it is too late. One of the cats sees him.
"Help!" Marcel thinks and climbs up a red curtain.

A moment later the cat starts climbing, too. Marcel can
hear it below him. He has to do something – and *fast*!
But what? Then he sees two candles above his head.
"That's the answer," he thinks.
He jumps onto the bookcase and starts to push the
candles over. They are very heavy, but in the end he does
it. Below him he hears, "Yeeooowwwww!"

"What's all that noise?" asks Antoine. "Look! The carpet's on *fire!*" says Henri. Spandini stands up. "Angelina! Quick, bring some water." Marcel looks over the bookcase. He can see the Mona Lisa on Spandini's desk. "OK," he thinks. "This is it." After that he runs down the curtain, across Spandini's desk, picks up the Mona Lisa, and runs out of the room.

Marcel runs for a long time. He thinks, "I want to leave the Mona Lisa somewhere safe. But where?" Then, after twenty minutes, he stops in a quiet street. In front of him there is a police station. The front door has a letter-box. "Of course!" Marcel thinks. "That's it." He stands up tall. Then he pushes the Mona Lisa through the letter-box.

Two days later Marcel is in Paris again. At the station he sees a newspaper. It says, 'ITALIAN POLICE FIND THE MONA LISA'. Then he goes to the Louvre and tells Céline everything. "Nine cats!" she says. "Oh Marcel, are you all right?" "Yes, I'm fine," Marcel answers. He goes to Céline's window. "And the Mona Lisa's fine, too. Look, Céline. She's smiling."

ACTIVITIES

Pages 1–7

Before you read

1   Read the Word List at the back of the book. What are the twenty
    words in your language? Find them in a dictionary.

2   Is it a famous place or a famous painting?

    a   Paris   **b**   The Louvre   **c**   The Mona Lisa

3   Look at the pictures in the book. What do you think?

    a   On pages 1–3, is it the morning or the evening?

    b   What is the man on page 3 doing?

    c   On page 5, is Marcel at an airport or a train station?

    d   Is he having a good dream or a bad dream on page 7?

While you read

4   Put the right word in the sentence.

    a   Céline's home is in the ....

    b   At 11 o'clock, Marcel says goodnight to ....

    c   He sees a thief. The thief .... the Mona Lisa.

    d   The thief puts the painting into a .... bag.

    e   .... jumps into the bag, too.

    f   The thief takes the bag to a train ....

    g   The thief's name is ....

    h   Marcel has a dream about ....

After you read

5   Answer the questions.

    a   How does the thief get into the Louvre at night?

    b   How does he steal the painting?

Before you read

6 Look at the pictures. What do you think?

    a Where is Marcel on page 8?

    b How many cats can you see on page 10?

    c Why are the cats running away on pages 12 and 13?

    d Where is the Mona Lisa on page 15?

While you read

7 What is first? What is after that? Write a number from 1 to 8 after
every sentence.

    a Marcel hides behind a chair.   .....

    b Two days later, the painting is back in Paris.   .....

    c The thieves go to Signor Spandini's house.   .....

    d Marcel goes to a police station in Venice.   .....

    e Signor Spandini says, "Quick, bring some water."   .....

    f The thieves arrive in Venice.   .....

    g Marcel pushes the Mona Lisa into a letter-box.   .....

    h Marcel climbs a red curtain.   .....

After you read

8 Why are they important in the story?

    a a black bag   **b** a red curtain   **c** a letter-box

9 You are Marcel inside the black bag on page 6. What are you
thinking? Write your answer.

10 Who are the people? Write your answers.

    a Antoine   **b** Henri   **c** Angelina   **d** Signor Spandini

WORD LIST *with example sentences*

candle (n) The lights aren't working. Put some *candles* on the table.

cat (n) *Cats* catch and eat small animals.

climb (v) Children often *climb* trees.

curtain (n) Open the *curtains* in front of that window.

desk (n) Our books are on the teacher's *desk*.

detective (n) Sherlock Holmes is a famous *detective*. He asks questions and catches bad people.

dream (v/n) All people *dream* at night, but I can never remember my *dreams* in the morning.

fire (n) There's a *fire* in the room. Bring water quickly!

guard (n) "Stop!" the *guard* says. "You can't go in there."

hide (v) Peter is *hiding* under the bed, and his mother can't see him.

inside (prep/adv) There's a bag on the table, and the money is *inside* it.

jump (v) Can you *jump* across the river?

letter-box (n) There are two or three letters in our *letter-box* every morning.

mouse (n) Marcel is a brown *mouse*. Some *mice* are white.

out (prep/adv) Go *out* of the house and walk across the road.

painting (n) Picasso's *paintings* are very famous and very expensive.

push (v) She *pushes* him, and he falls in the water.

Signor (n) English people say "Mr Smith". Italian people say "*Signor* Smith".

steal (v) He *steals* money from old people, and the police are looking for him.

thief (n) This *thief* steals cars. There are many car *thieves* in the town.

Pearson Education Limited
Edinburgh Gate, Harlow,
Essex CM20 2JE, England
and Associated Companies throughout the world.

ISBN: 978-1-4058-6955-3

First published 1991
New edition first published 1998
This edition first published 2008

5 7 9 10 8 6

Copyright © Longman Group Ltd 1991
This edition copyright © Pearson Education Ltd 2008
Illustrations by Inga Moore

Typeset by Graphicraft Ltd, Hong Kong
Set in 12/20pt Life Roman
Printed in China
SWTC/05

Published by Pearson Education Ltd in association with
Penguin Books Ltd, both companies being subsidiaries of Pearson Plc

For a complete list of the titles available in the Penguin Readers series please write
to your local Pearson Longman office or to: Penguin Readers Marketing Department,
Pearson Education, Edinburgh Gate, Harlow, Essex CM20 2JE, England.